Sometimes love

written by
Katrina Moore

illustrated by
Joy Hwang Ruiz

DIAL BOOKS FOR YOUNG READERS

Wobbly ears,

fuzz that's thick,

love is sometimes at first lick.

It's turning howls into a song,

a snuggle lasting all night long.

A bounce,

a pounce,

a tail that wiggles,

love is grass

that's rolled in giggles.

Sliding, scratching, through the halls,

love will sometimes break through walls.

It's clinging close and barrel hugs,

loading laundry, cleaning rugs.

Love is firm.

Love can bend.

Love knows how to be a friend.

Soft like whispers.

Sitting still.

Panting picks up speed until . . .

Salty tears. Sugar licks.

Weeping. Wailing. Throwing sticks.

Soft, yet *strong*, like hummingbirds,

love requires little words.

Pulling tight, barking no,

but sometimes love . . .

is letting go.

It's being brave when you feel shy.

It's starting small and saying "hi."

It's healing hurt by making art,

and holding paws inside your heart . . .

ready for a brand-new start.

Changes come . . .

and changes go.

Love through changes makes love *grow*.

Palms pressed tightly to the glass,

Counting minutes as they pass.

Pet Care for
Serving Soldiers

Sometimes love is coming home . . .

where love has stayed, where love has *grown*.

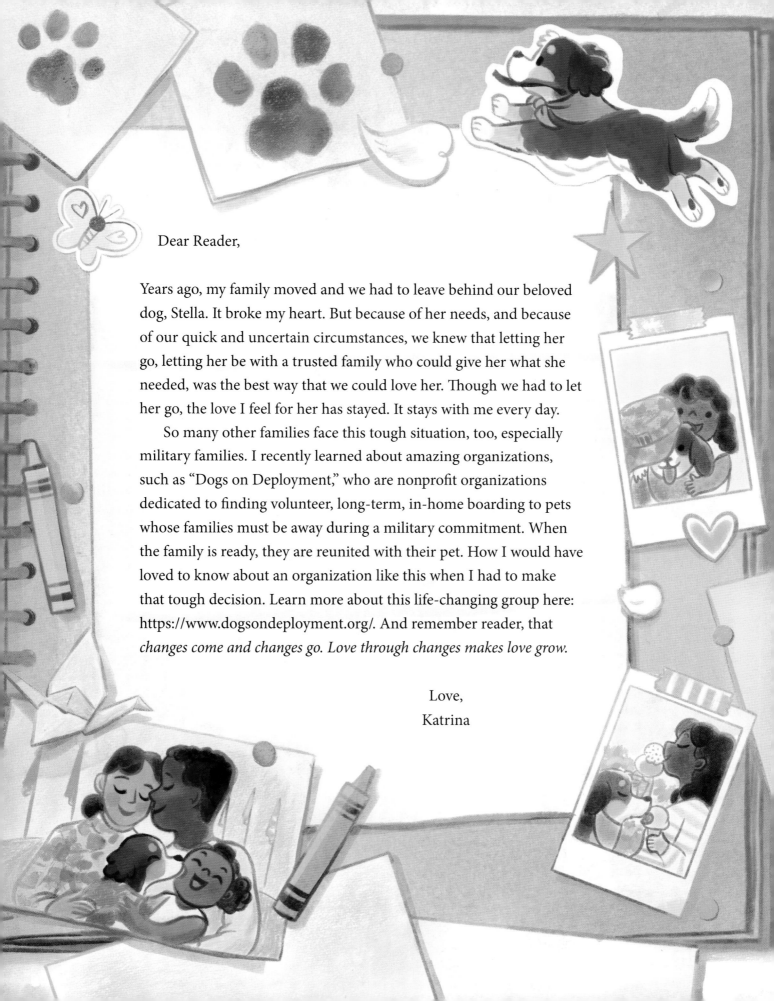

Dear Reader,

Years ago, my family moved and we had to leave behind our beloved dog, Stella. It broke my heart. But because of her needs, and because of our quick and uncertain circumstances, we knew that letting her go, letting her be with a trusted family who could give her what she needed, was the best way that we could love her. Though we had to let her go, the love I feel for her has stayed. It stays with me every day.

So many other families face this tough situation, too, especially military families. I recently learned about amazing organizations, such as "Dogs on Deployment," who are nonprofit organizations dedicated to finding volunteer, long-term, in-home boarding to pets whose families must be away during a military commitment. When the family is ready, they are reunited with their pet. How I would have loved to know about an organization like this when I had to make that tough decision. Learn more about this life-changing group here: https://www.dogsondeployment.org/. And remember reader, that *changes come and changes go. Love through changes makes love grow.*

Love,
Katrina

For Mom and Dad, I love you.
—K.M.

For readers everywhere —J.H.R.

Dial Books for Young Readers
An imprint of Penguin Random House LLC, New York

First published in the United States of America by Dial Books for Young Readers, an imprint of Penguin Random House LLC, 2022

Text copyright © 2022 by Katrina Moore
Illustrations copyright © 2022 by Jiae Hwang

Visit us online at penguinrandomhouse.com.

Library of Congress Cataloging-in-Publication Data is available.

Manufactured in China
ISBN 9780593323823
10 9 8 7 6 5 4 3 2 1
HH

Design by Jennifer Kelly • Text set in Minion Pro

The illustrations in this book were created digitally, with the help of ProCreate and help from all the dogs I got to pet on the street in research for this book.